CUENTO
DE LUZ

For Zaira, who's got it all: a pretty name, a big heart,
and now, a story dedicated to her.

*May children dream
like birds in flight.*

Zaira and the Dolphins

Text © 2011 Mar Pavon
Illustrations © 2011 Cha coco
This edition © 2011 Cuento de Luz SL
Calle Claveles 10 | Urb Monteclaro | Pozuelo de Alarcón | 28223 Madrid | Spain | www.cuentodeluz.com
Original title in Spanish: Zaira y los Delfines
English translation by Jon Brokenbrow

ISBN: 978-84-15241-65-2

Printed by Shanghai Chenxi Printing Co., Ltd. in PRC, July 2011, print number 1216-07

FSC
www.fsc.org
MIX
Paper from
responsible sources
FSC® C007923

Zaira
and the
Dolphins

Mar Pavon

Illustrated by Cha Coco

Just like she did every day, Zaira went to the
fountain in the square to see the dolphins.
She went with Spooky, her best friend.

"Look! The dolphins are playing! They're balancing balls on their noses!" gasped Zaira, absolutely thrilled.

Spooky smiled too, but all of the children who were in the square looked at them with strange expressions on their faces.

"Who are you talking to? What do you mean, the dolphins are playing? There's nothing in the fountain except water. And water doesn't play!"

Zaira and Spooky weren't listening. They were too busy watching the dolphins!

The next day after school, Zaira returned to her favorite place: the fountain in the square. This time, her boyfriend Indigo went with her.

"Look, Indigo!" she shouted with glee. "Today the dolphins are jumping as high as the water from the spout!"

Indigo admitted that it was a really amazing feat, but the children playing in the square looked on with puzzled expressions on their faces.

"Who's Indigo? And what dolphins are jumping? There's nothing in this fountain except water! And water doesn't jump!"

Instead of listening to them, Zaira and Indigo watched the dolphins and sat on the edge of the fountain with their arms around each other, just the way that boyfriends and girlfriends do.

Another afternoon, Zaira convinced her twin sister Gemma to come along with her to watch the dolphins.

"Can you hear the dolphins, Gemma? Today they're singing songs!"

Gemma clapped happily.
But the children who were playing around
them didn't understand anything.

"Who's Gemma? And where can you see
dolphins singing songs? There's nothing in
this fountain except water. And water sounds
like water!"

Zaira and Gemma didn't hear them—all they
wanted to listen to were the dolphins!

But one day, Zaira discovered that the fountain was empty. Some of the children, seeing the surprise on her face, made fun of her.

"Oh, what a pity! Dolphin Girl's run out of water!"
"And she's run out of dolphins!"
"What's the crazy little girl going to do now?
Maybe she'll go looking for whales in a puddle!"

All of the children who played in the square were laughing and jeering. But Zaira was about to burst into tears.

And then, all of a sudden, the fairy Takethat appeared in front of her, right in the middle of the fountain!

The first thing Takethat did was wipe the smiles off the faces of the children who were laughing at Zaira.

"Take that!" she said, proud of what she'd done.

At the same time, Zaira began to smile. Then the fairy asked her:
"Would you like to see some whales in a puddle?"

Unsure, Zaira said,
"Yes…well, no… well, I don't know…"

But her smile turned to laughter when Takethat asked her:
"Would you rather see your beautiful dolphins?"

"Oh yes!" said Zaira, "more than anything in the world!"

"Alright, then. The only thing you have to do is go home, behave yourself, and watch closely what's going on around you!"

Zaira obediently did everything Takethat had told her: she returned home, she behaved better than ever, and of course, she kept her eyes wide open all evening.

But the dolphins didn't appear. Zaira looked for them in the washbasin, in the toilet, in the watering can, in the kitchen sink, in a glass of water, and even in the mop bucket! But she couldn't find any sign of them.

Finally, it was bath time, something Zaira had hated since she was a baby.
But despite her protests, her Mom insisted on bathing her every day,
and that evening was no exception.

Suddenly, Zaira felt something bumping against her. There were two of them, and they were tickling her tummy so much that she couldn't stop giggling.

"Goodness me, Zaira, I've never seen you enjoy bath time so much!" said Mom with surprise.

Finally, the dolphins let her come up for air. Zaira made the most of the opportunity, and shouted:

"Spooky! Indigo! Gemma! Come and see the dolphins! They're here with me in the bath, and they're tickling me!"

"I didn't know there were so many of us in this house!" laughed Mom, as she tried to wash Zaira.

But Zaira was too busy splashing around and giggling.

And just then, a certain fairy took
the opportunity to wipe the steam off the
mirror with her wand, see her reflection,
and, with a wink in her eye, say in a very
satisfied voice:

"Take that!"